ALICE PROVENSEN

VIKING

Alice Provensen

For Erik, Elisa, Beth, and Ethan Provensen

and now, of course, for Sean Martin Mitchell,

with love

—A.P.

The art for *Punch in New York*
was prepared in oil and ink on vellum.

VIKING
Published by the Penguin Group
Viking Penguin, a division of Penguin Books USA Inc.,
375 Hudson Street, New York, New York 10014, U.S.A.
Penguin Books Ltd, 27 Wrights Lane, London W8 5TZ, England
Penguin Books Australia Ltd, Ringwood, Victoria, Australia
Penguin Books Canada Ltd, 2801 John Street, Markham, Ontario, Canada L3R 1B4
Penguin Books (N.Z.) Ltd, 182-190 Wairau Road, Auckland 10, New Zealand

Penguin Books Ltd, Registered Offices: Harmondsworth, Middlesex, England

First published in 1991 by Viking Penguin, a division of Penguin Books USA Inc.

1 3 5 7 9 10 8 6 4 2

A ROSY LAYER OF SMOG hangs over New York City as the Flight from London prepares for its descent into Kennedy Airport. On board, Il Professore Tucci-Piccini is fussing over his customs declaration and wondering if his puppets need green cards to work in America. His bags are bursting with the cast of his famous Punch and Judy show—the Crocodile and the Baby, the Devil and the Hangman, Judy and the little dog Toby, the Black Man, the Baker, the Cop, and the Clown.

In the International Arrivals Building, the Professore shows his Visitor's
Visa to the Passport Control Police. He explains to them that his name
is pronounced *Too-chee Peach-eeny*, but he knows they will never get
it right. Now the Customs Inspector wants to paw through all the
Professore's suitcases.

Professore Tucci-Piccini argues with him. He is afraid his puppets will be lost, will stray or be stolen. Indeed, even as the argument goes on, a Bad Thief, disguised as a porter, is stealing the most important bag of all — the one containing the Star of the Show — Mr. Punch, with his pointed hat and his wooden bat.

The Bad Thief and his buddy, the Cabbie, hurry over the bridge to their den in Manhattan. They are sure the suitcase is full of Money!

The Thief and his Gang open the suitcase. Out pops Mr. Punch. "A DOLL!" snarls the Leader. Sneering, he throws Mr. Punch out the window of the fortieth floor.

Down

    down

        down

           falls

             Mr. Punch,

          right into

      the bucket

         of a

            Window

          Washer!!

SPLASH!

Down

    down

        down.

Down

   down

      Mr. Punch

     slides,

down

   the

     Window

       Washer's

     rope

all the way

    to

      the street.

He lands

    right

     on

   a

    beautiful…

…Wedding Cake! "MUGGER! POLICE!" cries the Baker Man.
"Thank you for a safe landing, Signore," says Mr. Punch.

"ROOTY-TO-TOO-IT!" he shouts as he sets off on his own.

Adrift and alone in the big city, Mr. Punch soon loses his way.
"Oh, so tired," he whimpers, "no place to sit."

At last! Mr. Punch sees a place to sit down.

TOO LATE! A Nasty Man grabs the seat quick.
"You got something to say, Punk?" he says to Mr. Punch.

Mr. Punch is quick on his feet.
"OH, NO!" says the Nasty Man.
"THAT'S THE WAY TO DO IT!" shouts Mr. Punch.

And he is on his way.
Now Mr. Punch is hungry.
So hungry!

Mr. Punch: "Here is my penny."
Hot Dog Man: "PENNY?"
Boy: "You nuts, Mac?"

Mr. Punch: "You won't give me a sausage?"
Hot Dog Man: "No sausidge for no penny!"
Boy: "Yum."

Mr. Punch: "Ha!"
Hot Dog Man: "Oh no!"
Boy: "Chomp."

Hot Dog Man: "HIPPY! FREAK! POLICE!"
Mr. Punch: "Just like in the old country."
Boy: "BURP."

A Policeman sees Mr. Punch running away. He blows his whistle!

Out from an open manhole cover comes a big green Crocodile.
"GOTCHA!" he says.

"OOF!"

Waiting for
a passing tourist
is a band of muggers.
Mr. Punch walks right into their arms.

Mr. Punch is not afraid.
"See, Friends, no money," he says.

"Come with me, Pals. I will lead you to GOLD!"
Mr. Punch knows how to deal with rascals.

Says Mr. Punch, "We must bait our hook to catch our fish, Boys." Parked by the curb

is a Beautiful Car. It belongs to Mr. Harry Helmstrump, the Richest Man in the World.

Mr. Punch writes a Naughty Word on the Beautiful Car with his spray can while

Mr. Helmstrump's Chauffeur, James, rises to the bait. "CREEP!" he shouts.

the rascally muggers make themselves invisible. "Way to go!" they whisper.

He follows Mr. Punch right into the hands of the Rascals.

Mr. Punch puts on the Chauffeur's hat and gets into the driver's seat.
The muggers drape themselves secretly on the car.
"Home, James," says Mr. Helmstrump.

"Yes, SIR!" says Mr. Punch.
Mr. Punch has never driven a car before. Off they go!
The wicked Rascals bounce off the Beautiful Car as it rides over a Patrol Car.

"You are a good driver, James,"
says Mr. Helmstrump.

"Thank you, Sir,"
says Mr. Punch.

Bounce

   Bounce

Rumble

   Bumble

      Thumpety

         Bumpety

   Bump

   Bump

   SQUASH!

The Beautiful Car sags

gently to the street.

''No tea today, thank you, James,''

says Mr. Helmstrump.

"Where is James, my man?"
"James took sick, Sir," says Mr. Punch. "I am James's cousin, Punch."
"Then you may drive for me, Punch. I'll call you James."
"Aye, aye, Sir," says Mr. Punch.

Mr. Punch has conquered New York! He has a steady job. He drives a big car.
He lives in a mansion. But somehow he is sad and lonely. He wonders
what has happened to Professore Tucci-Piccini and all his puppet friends.
He misses his little dog, Toby. Mr. Punch is beginning to feel sorry for himself.

One day
as Mr. Punch is
driving through the Park
on his way to buy
a cigar for
Mr. Helmstrump,
he sees a Puppet Theater
surrounded by
a group of children.

It is the theater of
Il Signore Professore
TUCCI-PICCINI!
and Judy!
and the Baby!
and the little dog,
Toby!

"Yo!"
yells the Black Man.

"Hang Five!"
hollers the Hangman.

"Well, look what the cat
dragged in!"
sniggers Satan.

"Far out!"
says the Clown.

"Macaroni,"
murmurs Il Professore.

"Pop!"
goes the Baby.

"Yap! Yap!"
yaps the little dog, Toby.

TOGETHER AT LAST!

"Hurrah!"
the children shout.

Now they all work for Mr. Helmstrump
six days a week—and they rip him off good.
Sundays, Professore Tucci-Piccini's
Puppet Theater performs in the Park… FOR FREE!

In the fifteenth century in Italy a new form of secular drama emerged. Known as the *commedia dell'arte*, it was a theater, traditionally "professional, unliterary, improvised, ambulant, and played by stock characters." The Punch and Judy show is probably the sole surviving example of true popular theater in the commedia dell'arte tradition. The puppet Punch is one of the wickedest characters ever to grow out of it.

Punch triumphs over everything that is civilized and honest and legal, everything that is good and kind and humane. For hundreds of years he has foiled the authorities, betrayed his friends, and abused his wife. Over and over again he has thrown his baby out the window of his impoverished theater.

Punch is sly. He is petulant. He is a liar. He is vulgar. Punch is ugly. He has no redeeming features. And it is with these disagreeable qualities that we secretly identify.

There is no point in moralizing about Mr. Punch's behavior on his mean little stage. His crimes and misdemeanors are committed to show us the dark side of our own natures. To present Punch in a reformed version would not enable us to recognize our own amoral tendencies, nor give us insight into our own repressions.

Trapeze artists let us experience danger vicariously, and roller coasters allow the luxury of fear without the terror of imminent destruction. A Punch and Judy show, with its crude, brawling folk tradition, permits us to look at our own dark thoughts. By facing them and laughing at them, we are better able to handle our own aggressions and control our antisocial behavior. Punch provides us with a harmless outlet for our guilty thoughts.

Punch doesn't motivate us to *do* evil deeds. Frightening as *his* behavior can be, we find *ourselves* glad the baby is always on hand for the next performance.

—Alice Provensen